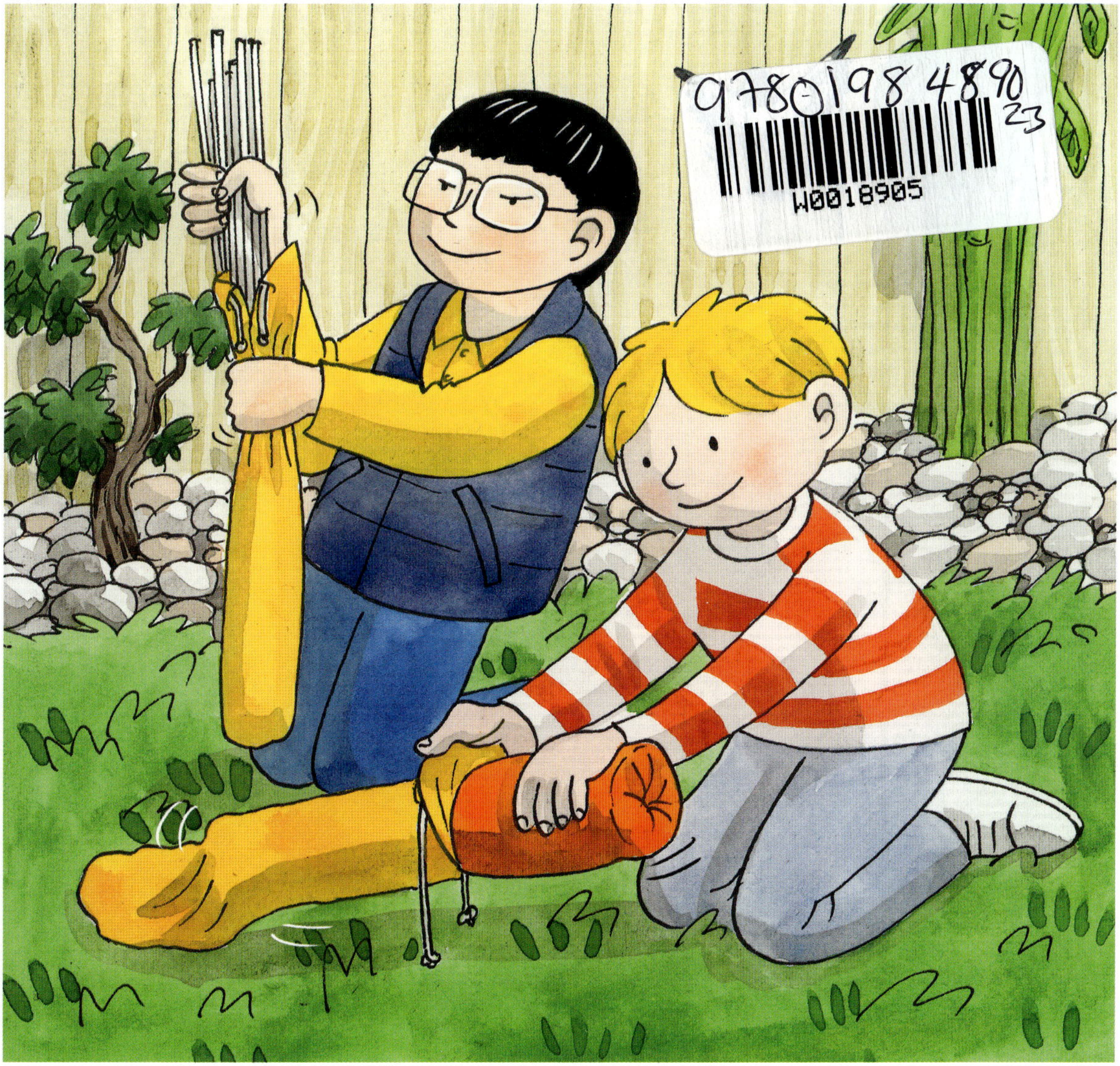

Lee and Kipper had a tent.

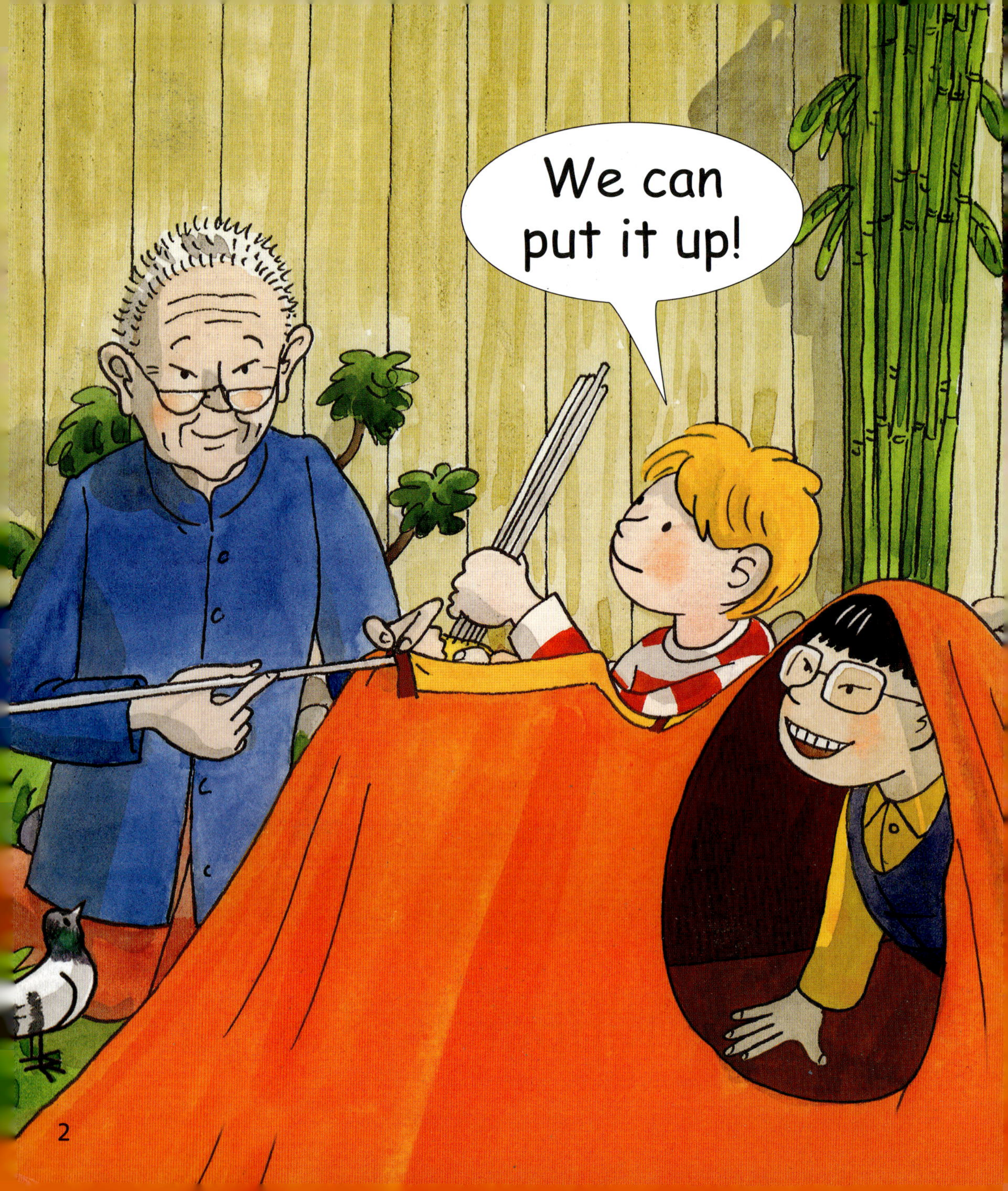
We can put it up!

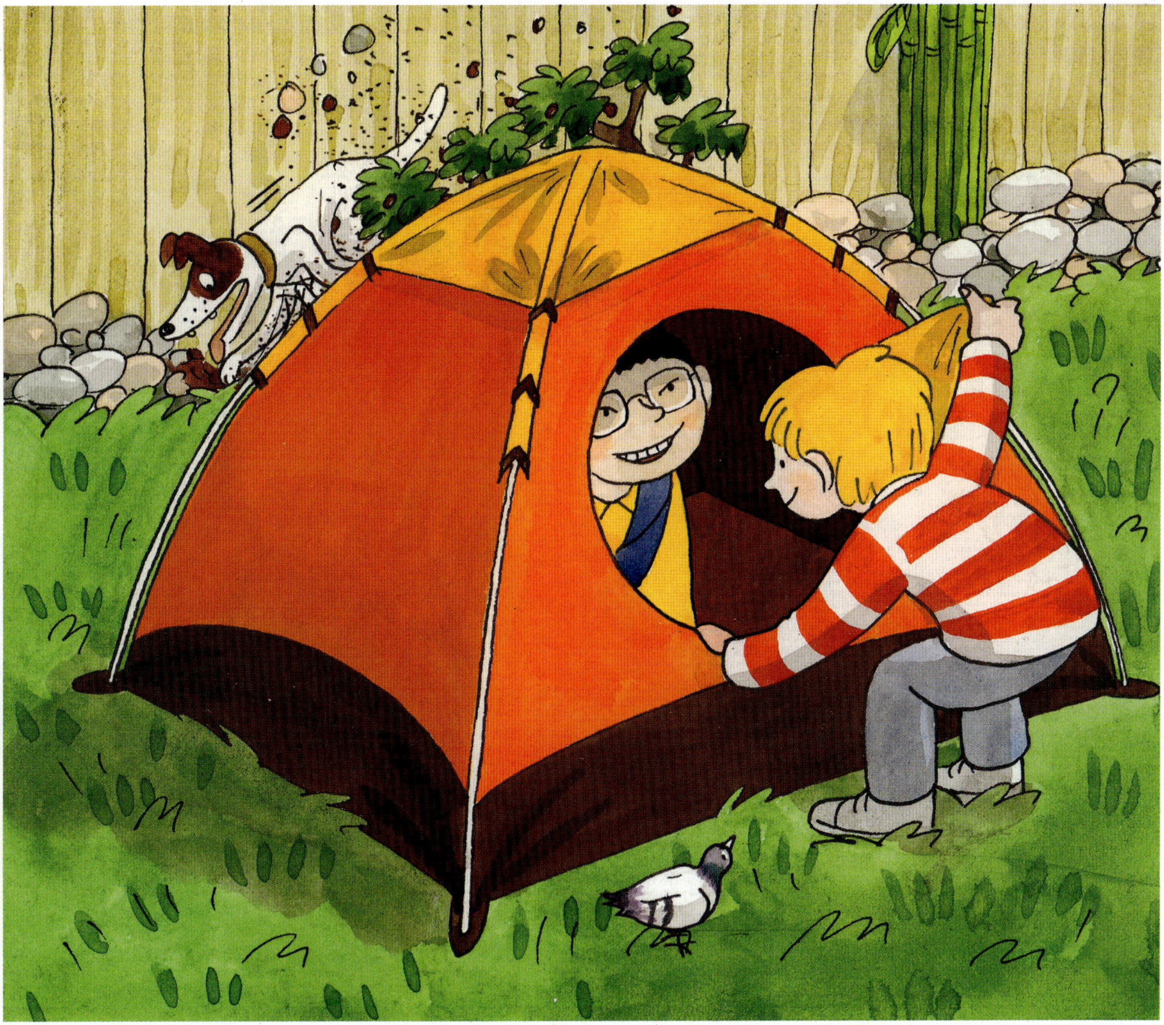

Lee and Kipper had fun
in the tent.

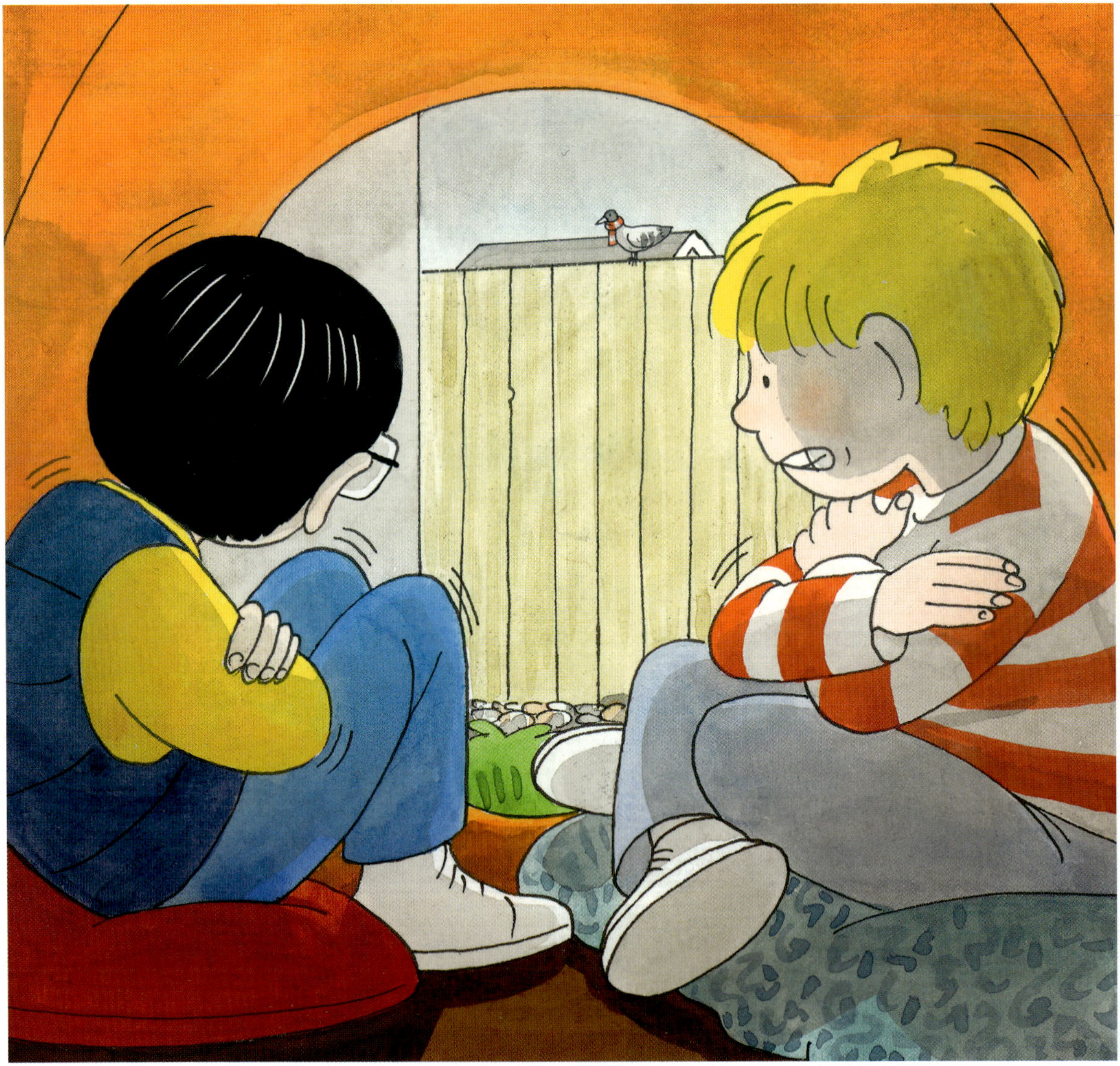

It got cold . . .

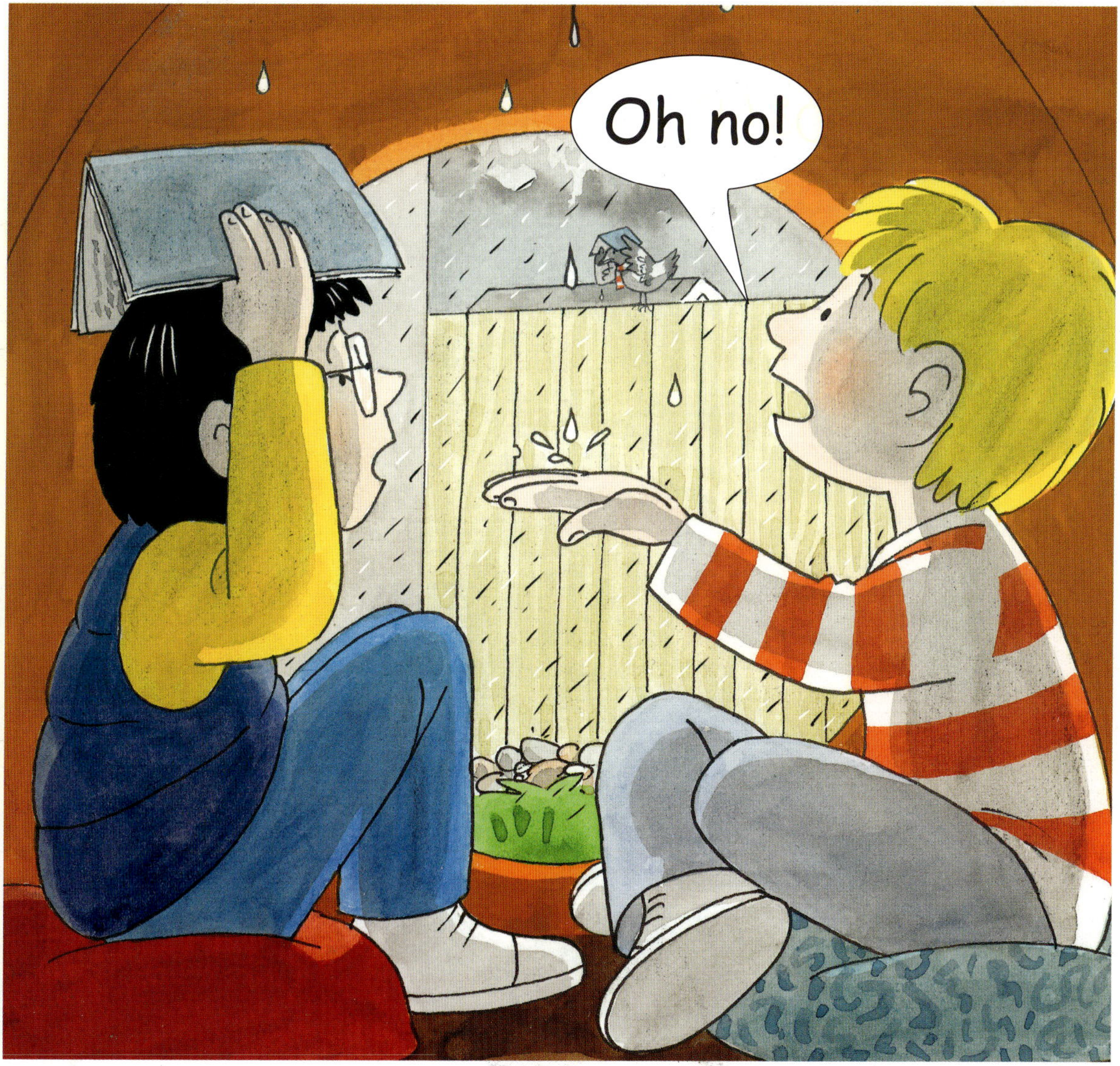

. . . and it got wet.

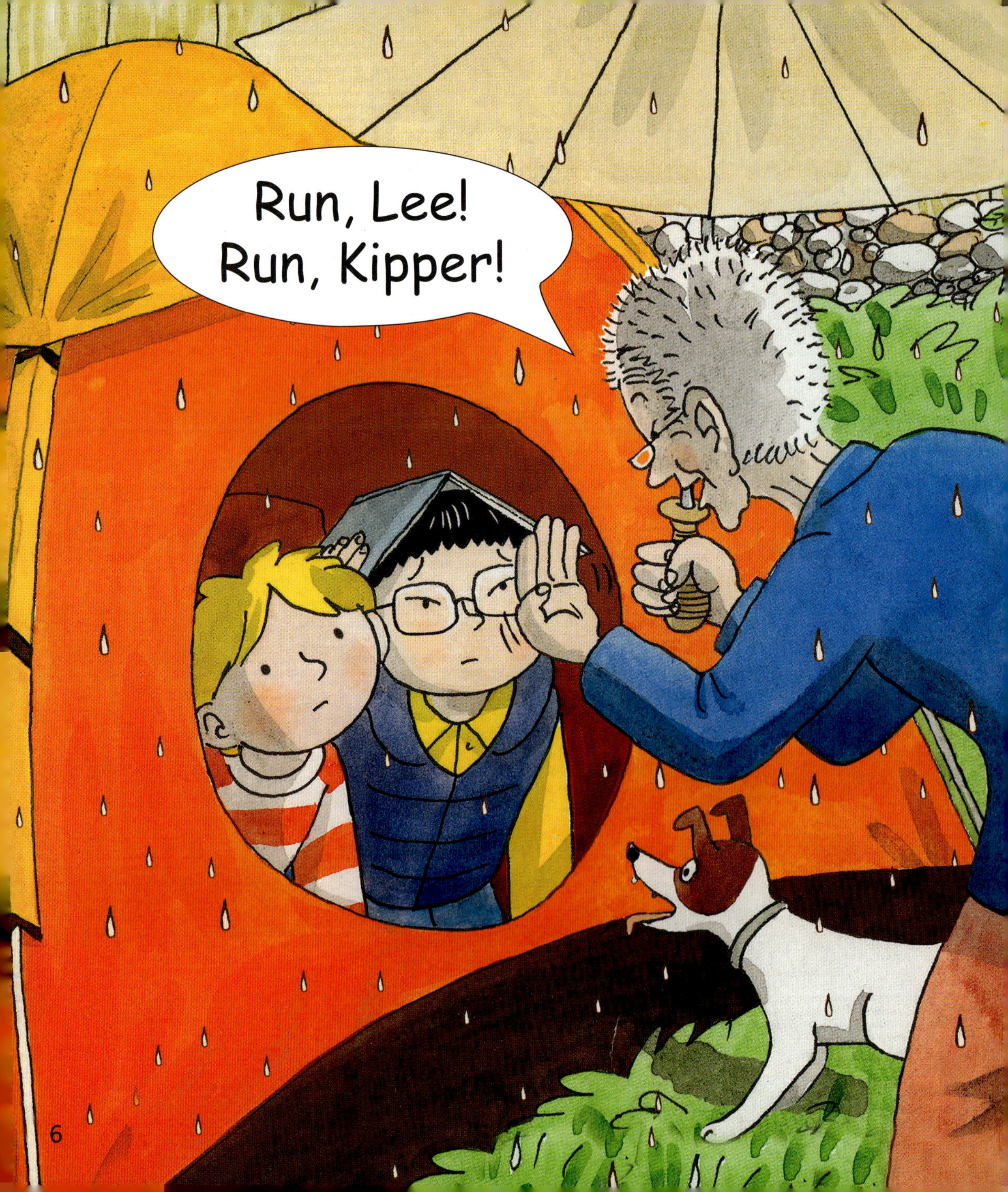
Run, Lee!
Run, Kipper!

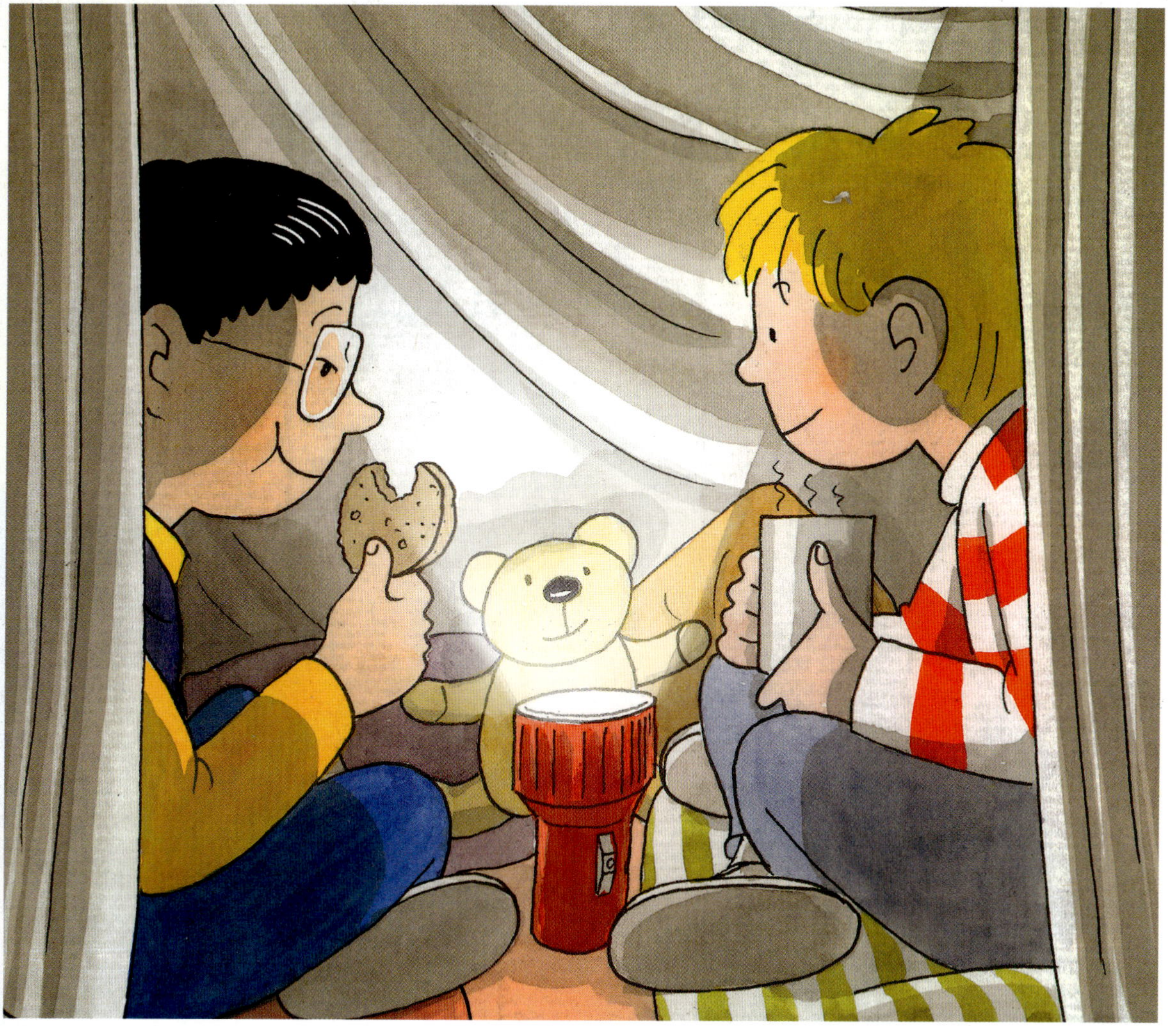

It was a lot of fun in
the tent.

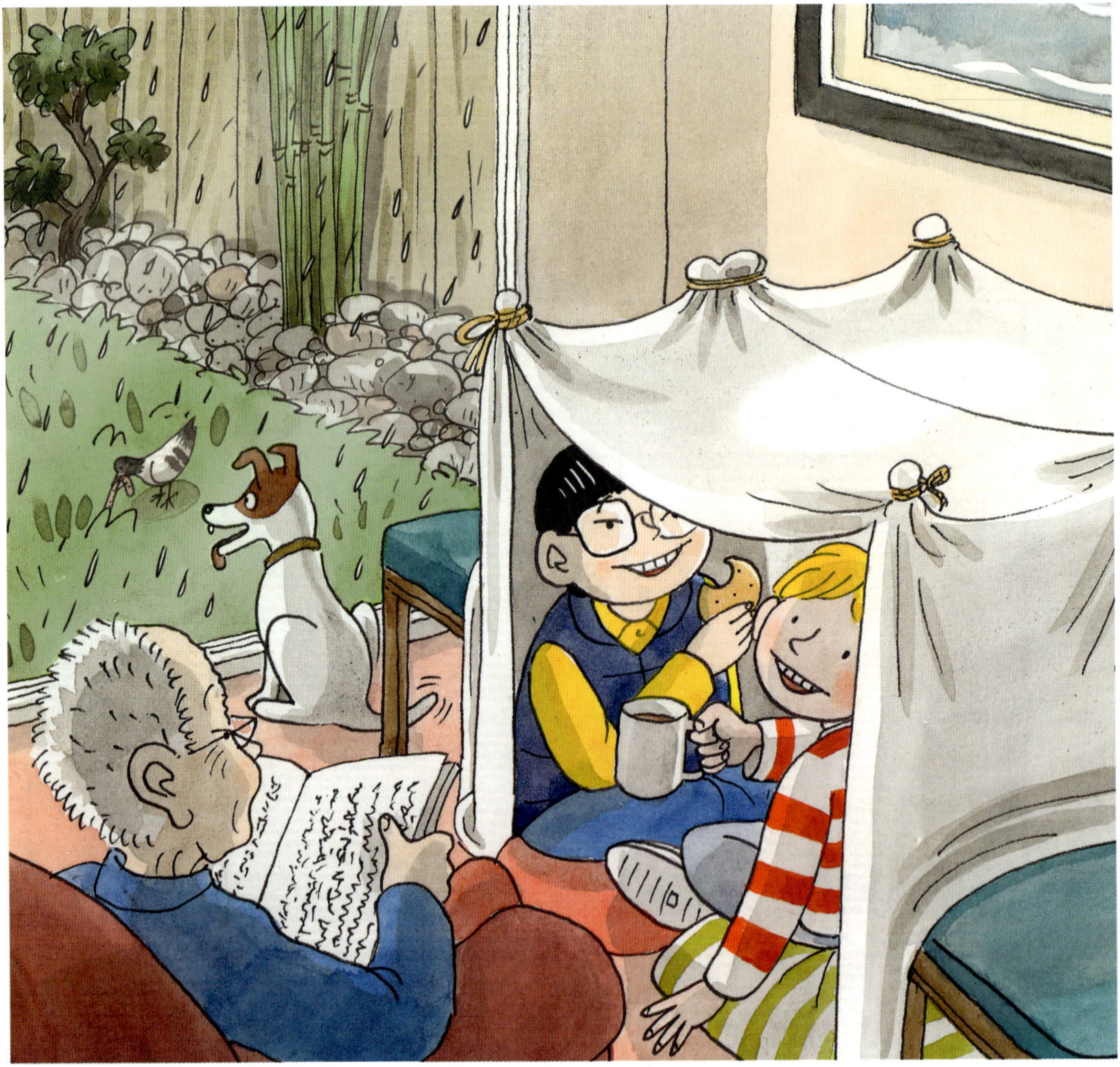

It was not cold and wet!